The Courageous Children

Semaj S. Hickman

authorHOUSE®

AuthorHouse™
1663 Liberty Drive
Bloomington, IN 47403
www.authorhouse.com
Phone: 1 (800) 839-8640

Published by AuthorHouse   10/12/2016

ISBN: 978-1-5246-4487-1 (sc)
ISBN: 978-1-5246-4486-4 (e)

Print information available on the last page.

This book is printed on acid-free paper.

Acknowledgement

I love all of my teachers and family members and as much as I would like to single handily take credit for this book. There are some people I would love shout out and here is a short list of them my wonderful mother Ronda Nelson for standing by me and supporting my dream, my awesome father who always encourages me to follow my dreams Lawrence Hickman, my amazing brother who is my partner in crime who pulled out time to help me spell check and make corrections Ja'Ron Nelson, my principal who helps educate me at Pourpard Elementary Mrs. Penny Stocks, and of course all of the teachers who taught me but especially Mrs. Julie VanTol my amazing kindergarten teacher who noticed my love and talent for reading and writing from the very start.

Chapter 1

The Kids

THERE ONCE WERE TWO GIRLS their names were Violet and Kaitlin. Violet was a tall 18-year-old girl who had blonde hair and pale skin Kaitlin was a shorter girl with brown curly hair she was 16. Oh and did I mention the to girls were homeschooled.

Unfortunately neither one of the girls had a chance to meet their mom, she ran away after they were born and the father worked at a manufacturing company in a suburban city right out of Detroit. They were all middle-class citizens. But one day their father was a caught tax invading and went to jail for 20 years.

Kaitlin and Violet survived off the money their father left in their bank count. But after six months all the money drained out. And the two girls ended up living in a shelter in Detroit. They stayed there for six weeks until they went out on the search for a new home where a loving family would take them in as if they were their own. They searched for 2 hours they survived of food and water they stored up before they left the shelter.

"I see a house not too far from here "Violet said happily. "I hope this family is willing to take us in "Kaitlin said. Ding dong the doorbell rang as the two girls stared at the door. "Can I help you to girls?" A nice woman said. "Yes we are homeless and we were wondering if you're willing to take this in for a couple of months until we can find a permanent home? "Violet said. "Absolutely, please come in "the nice woman said. "My husband's taking a nap, my name is Katie what are your names?" Katie asked "Well my name is Violet I'm 18 and my little sister Kaitlin is 16, "Violet said.

"Thank you again for taking us and you are very kind "Kaitlin said. "You're absolutely welcome" Katie said. "I was actually just prepare dinner are you girls hungry? "Katie asked. "Yes "both the girl said anxiously.

3

After they all ate they were very tired so they headed off to sleep and so did the husband and wife. Early that morning Katie kindly made breakfast for her, her husband, Kaitlin, and Violet. "Where are you girls from you certainly look like you're not from here" Katie's husband Albert said. "We were from the suburban city right outside of Detroit but when our dad was caught tax invading he was arrested and is now in jail for 20 years, and we never got to meet our mom she ran away after we were born my father had money in his bank account but for us to pay the mortgage, buy groceries, and pay the electric bill and of course we both bought bikes so we can go from place to place especially me because I had to go to work every day but after six months all the money in our father's bank account was all used up." Violet said in a shy voice.

"I'm actually looking for work now and I've just given my Resume to a restaurant that caters special events such as wedding receptions, graduations and birthday parties. And they pay a lot of money so if I get this job will probably only be here for about 6 months if I can find and inexpensive house back in the suburbs. "Violet said. "You have a very beautiful house and the room with the two separate beds that you gave us is absolutely amazing "Kaitlin said thankfully. "Thank you" the kind couple said.

After breakfast they all sat down and got to know each other a little better. By the time they were finished it was 10o'clock so they all ate lunch and watched tv till they all went off to sleep. Early that morning about an hour after sunrise Kaitlin heard the sound of the bouncy ball hitting the ground. She got up and looked out of the window, and she saw a tall dark skin boy who looked about her age and had straight slick hair and really nice clothes. Wow he's cute Kaitlin thought. So she threw on some clothes and went outside to go talk to the boy.

"Hello "Kaitlin said to the boy. "Hello my name is Logan and I'm 16" Logan said. "Me and my sister live with that family across the street," Kaitlin said. And they talk for at least an hour. They agreed that Logan's brother, Kaitlin's sister, Logan, and Kaitlin would all go bike riding the next day.

When Kaitlin went back home Violet was already awake Katie and Albert agreed to take both of the girls clothes shopping since the only close they had were all dirty and messed up. When they all got back home the girls had about 29 new outfits they were all gorgeous one of Kaitlin's outfits had pink rhinestones on the shirt and pink jogging pants. And one of violet outfit had a purple shirt with pants that said Era Postal on both of the legs. The next day Violet, Kaitlin, Logan, and Logan's brother Alex all went bike riding Violet and Alex talked for a little while so did Kaitlin in the Logan. She is so smart and cute I really like Kaitlin, Logan thought. I really like Logan, Kaitlin thought.

Alex is amazing, Violet thought. Violet is awesome, Alex thought. "Can I get your number so we could stay in touch?" Alex said to Violet and Logan said to Kaitlin. "Yes" Kaitlin and Violet said.

They all went home. And got a good nights sleep. The next day Violet found out she got the catering job. She was so happy. Mean while Kaitlin called Logan and they talked on the phone for a rough 30 minutes.

They agreed to go on a date at 7:00. Kaitlin wore a gorgeous blue dress and adorable silver heels. And Logan wore a black tux with a white bow tie. They had an amazing time they went to a movie. Then went home and went to sleep.

September 28, 2004 was a terrific day for Kaitlin and Violet Newpower. The next day Violet woke up at 6:00 sharp to go to work. And Kaitlin woke up at 12:24 PM and called Logan. They talked about there date. They enjoyed there date so much they decided to go on another date on Tuesday (It was Monday).

After work Violet was so worn out she went straight to sleep. Katie and Albert woke Violet so that she can eat dinner. After that they let her rest peacefully. Then it was 9 o'clock so they all set off to sleep. The next day at 6 o'clock Violet went to work.

And at 12:00 AM Kaitlin went off on her date she wore a beautiful shirt a pink and purple pants and sandals with pink rhinestones. Logan wore an all white tux with a black tie. This time they went out to dinner. "Kaitlin, Logan, what are you doing here? "Violet said.

"What a what a coincidence we came to the same restaurant you work at, me and Logan are actually on a date, our second date." Kaitlin said. "Well what can I get you" Violet asked. "Well I'm not hungry like that so I'll just take the fries and mandarin oranges "Kaitlin said. "I'll have with the beautiful lady is having," Logan said.

After Kaitlin and Logan ate they talked for about 30 minutes. Then they went home. About 15 minutes after Kaitlin got home Violet came home from work. Violet talked to Kaitlin and teased her about dating Logan. At dinner Katie and Albert asked how Kaitlin and Violets day was.

And they told them about Logan and Alex. That night Violet called Alex and they agreed after Alex got off work which was at 12:00 PM and after Violet got off work which is also at 12:00 PM they would go on a date. Violet was so excited she really really liked Alex and Alex really really liked her. She decided she was going to wear a purple dress with rhinestones around the waist with purple rhinestone heels. Alex decided he was going to wear a blue tux with a white tie.

By the time they got home it was late so everybody went to sleep. That morning it was raining and until it stopped raining Violet wasn't positive if she was going to work. So she woke up before everybody and made breakfast for her, Alex, Kaitlin, Logan, Katie, and Albert. Then she woke everybody up in the house and then went across street and woke Logan and Alex up and ask their mom if they could come over and thankfully they're mom said yes. So Katie, Albert, Alex, and Logan all got to know each other a little better and Katie and Albert felt a lot better about Violet going on a dates with Alex and Kaitlin going on dates with Logan. After breakfast Kaitlin and Logan went out bike riding and so did Violet and Alex. They had an amazing time.

After that Violet and Alex went home to change and went on their date. Then Violet asked Alex if he could drive her past a house that she's looking into buying that in the suburbs. She heard it was really inexpensive and big. Alex of course agreed to go check out the house. After that Alex drove Violet home. "Alex I really like you, "Violet said. "Violet I really like you to," Alex said. And the most amazing thing happened...

Chapter 2

The Kiss

... THEY KISSED! WHEN VIOLET went inside she told Kaitlin all about it. Violet and Alex didn't talk for two weeks straight until Violet decided to call Alex. They agreed to go out to brunch together to talk about the kiss. When they got there they both said down and began there talk.

"Violet I really like you and I think you should take this to the next level I would like you to be my girlfriend, "Alex said in a shy voice. "Absolutely" Violet said. After that Alex and Violet went home. "Kaitlin me and Alex are officially dating, "Violet said, "OMG that's terrific I wish Logan and asked me to be his girlfriend "Kaitlin replied. "I'm sure you will he's probably just waiting for the right time "Violet said supportively.

"Do you know what I'm going to call him right now and ask if you wants to go out to lunch with me, hey Logan I was wondering if you wanted to go to lunch with me in five minutes, OK awesome see you then "Kaitlin said excitedly. When Kaitlin and Logan met up for brunch Logan said the most meaningful heartwarming words a boy could ever say to a girl..." "Kaitlin will you be my girlfriend ". "I would love to, Kaitlin replied excitedly. After that they kissed, it was the most heartwarming amazing kiss. "I'll call you later, "Logan said.

And they both went home, Kaitlin told Violet all about the kiss. After that they decided to make dinner for Katie and Albert. "This is an amazing dinner and I'm thankful for it," Katie and Albert said thankfully. They all watched TV for about 25 minutes then they headed off to sleep. Earlier that morning Violet woke up and told Katie that Albert that her and Kaitlin would only be staying there for a few more months.

Because she found a nice house that was inexpensive and should be able to buy herself a car with the extra money that she would save up. Katie and Albert were happy for her and a little upset. After that Violet left out for work. And Kaitlin stayed at home with Katie and Albert, they all talked and laughed they had a very nice bonding experience. Katie Albert when me and Violet move I will call and come over as much as I can." Kaitlin said.

But Kaitlin could still tell by the look in Katie and Alberts eyes that they would miss her and Violet dearly. When Violet got home her and Kaitlin went across the street and told Logan and Alex about them moving soon "Don't worry will visit as much as we can and we can always call and text each," Kaitlin and Violet told Logan and Alex. "Well we should spend as

much time together as we can before you move,"
Alex and Logan told Violet and Kaitlin. And
they did just that, that night Kaitlin, Logan,
Violet, and Alex went on a double date. "I'm
having an amazing time, "Kaitlin told Logan.

After their double date Kaitlin and Violet
went over Logan and Alex's house so that
Logan and Alex's parents get a chance to meet
Kaitlin and Violet. "Kaitlin our parents don't,
don't like you and Violet so me and you can't
date anymore" Logan told Kaitlin and Alex told
Violet. Kaitlin and Violet cried their hearts out.
The two girls told Katie and Albert. They felt
terrible.

So they all baked cookies for Alex's and
Logan's parents to try and change their minds.
Unfortunately it didn't work. That night Kaitlin

and Violet had similar dreams that they were on an island it was beautiful and they were smelling the ocean breeze it was amazing until they both saw Alex and Logan's face appeared in the sky and they said "I'm breaking up with you". Then they both woke up and shared the similar dream this with each other. They cried them self's to sleep.

That morning Kaitlin and Violet decided to get over Alex and Logan. After Violet went to work Kaitlin made Albert, Katie, and herself some blue berry pancakes. "Mmm" Albert said. "You should get a job as a cook" Katie said. "Thanks I might consider sending in my resume" Kaitlin said.

"Maybe you could get a job at the same place as Violet?" Katie suggested. You know what I'm going to go send in my resume right now," Kaitlin said excitedly. And she left. When she got there, there was still a job opening.

So she gave them her resume and they told her to be at the interview on Friday that week. (It was Thursday). She was so excited she told Albert and Katie. The all waited on Violet to get home so they could spread the good news. 3 Hours Later "Violet I'm going to apply for the cooking spot at your job" Kaitlin exclaimed.

"Awesome" Violet said excitedly. After that they eat lunch watch TV until dinner time then they went to sleep. Kaitlin was so excited for have a job interview so she get a break and went out to the interview. When interview was done Kaitlin went home and waited about an hour then she got a call that said...

Chapter 3

You Got The Job

... "YOU GOT THE JOB. "The manager Pete said. "Oh my God, Katie, Albert, Violet I got the job."" Oh my god that's awesome "Katie Albert and Violet said. They made cake and celebrated it was an amazing day.

After the celebration they talked about the job for hours. They were all so happy for her. They all slept amazingly. Kaitlin and Violet woke up at 5:40 A.M., and made breakfast for everyone, then ate and went to work they were so excited. When she got there she got straight to work. Meanwhile Katie and Albert waited anxiously for the girls to get off work.

After a long tiring day of work the girls told Katie and Albert all about it. It was amazing, everybody was so nice and sincere. ""Work there as long as I have and see if it's the same ha ha, no I'm just kidding." They said happily. And all rested peacefully especially Kaitlin and Violet, they were incredibly tired. And they continued to do that exact routine for months, but after so long the girls finally earned enough money to buy a house and a car for Violet. It was hard to tell Katie and Albert they were moving out, "Katie Albert this is not easy to tell you but we found a big 2 bedroom house that is extremely cheap and with some of the money we'll have left over I'll be able to buy a car, me and Kaitlin checked it out and we decided to...

Chapter 4

Moving Out

WE DECIDED TO MOVE OUT, "Violet said "Well as heartbreaking as this is we are extremely happy for you, but let us know if you need anything," Katie said supportively. "I agree," Albert said. "We will visit all the time, and we are buying the house on Tuesday (It was Sunday). So we should be out of here by Wednesday, "Kaitlin said sadly but also happily. Kaitlin and Violet told Katie and Albert more about the house.

Katie and Albert were so supportive Kaitlin and Violet. "Tomorrow will it be OK if me and Albert stop by and check out the house "Katie said. "I think that would be a great idea, "Violet said. Kaitlin had been very quiet. I know my sister and it's been like her to be this quiet somethings wrong but I can't put my finger on it, Violet that.

Violet said nothing but boy was she anxious to find out what was wrong with Kaitlin. But what she didn't know was Kaitlin didn't want to move I mean she did but Katie and Albert were her family. But she continued to think on the bright side. After that Violet and Kaitlin went over to save their goodbyes to the boys. Then they got a good nights rest so that they could be up and anxious for the morning.

That morning they all work up took a shower set on some clothes and got in the car so they could go check at the house. They were all so anxious and excited. When they got there Katie and Albert love the outside. "Let's see if the inside is is beautiful as the outside," Albert said. They went inside and when they saw the house it was so humongous and beautiful.

It had 2 huge bedrooms, and in the living room was a flatscreen TV and beautiful red velvet couch, In the kitchen there were marble counters, and in the bedroom there were two queen size bed with no sheets or covers because they wanted it to be your choice. The house was just beautiful. After Violet, Kaitlin, Katie and Albert admired The house they went home Katie and Albert talked while Violet and Kaitlin Packed. By the time they finished it was 11:00 and they knew they had to wake up early to meet the seller and move in. Early that morning Kaitlin woke up super early and made when Violet woke up she noticed breakfast is made and Kaitlin was sitting in the living room watching TV she asked Kaitlin was there something on her mind, Kaitlin said no, even though she was still a little upset about having to leave.

But she knew she was going to visit every chance she got so she stayed on the positive side. And finally believed her because she was a lot better than she was the day before. After they ate the girls went out to go meet the seller when they got there there was a little surprise waiting for them...

Chapter 5

The House

WHEN THE GIRLS GOT TO the house there was little surprise waiting for them... there old middle school friend Penelope was the seller.

Penelope = amazing best friend, super smart, and has the memory of a donkey. "Oh my God Penelope you're selling this house, "both of the girls said in the excitement. "Kaitlin Violet is that you "Penelope asked. The three girls ran up to each other hugging they were so happy to see each other, but at the same time angry they didn't stay in touch.

They exchange numbers and Penelope help the girls move-in but unfortunately she had plans so she had to leave. But they were still so happy to see her. They were so happy to finally be able to buy a house of course and still a little sad that they wouldn't to be seeing Katie and Albert every day but still very often of course so they kept their thoughts on the good side of that equation. After that they did a little side shopping like the groceries, covers and sheets for their beds. Both girls decided to get black, Red, and pink pillows, sheets, and covers for their beds. And for the groceries juice, pot pies, Pop, and etc.

You know just get the hang of it. And when they went to sleep peacefully after all of that moving and grooving they were worn out. Then before she went to bed Violet set an alarm clock for 10:30 AM so she could go look for her new car. And what was awesome about the house they bought was the fact that they had so much leftover money Violet could buy a car and still have enough money to live on. Early that morning at 10:30 AM finally woke up and started searching cars.

And when Kaitlin woke up she made herself an amazing, delicious, and savory omelet that she made with eggs, squash, and baby spinach. Then she decided to call Katie but no answer so she called again but still no answer so she called Albert but no answer. "Their probably doing something" Kaitlin said to herself. So she decided to watch some TV when she turned on the TV streams breaking news alert appeared, so Kaitlin turned on the news. And when she flipped to the news she saw something so devastating, heartbreaking, and mood wrecking. And do you know what she saw...?

When she flipped to the news do you know what she saw...? Albert on the news "A man named Albert Angus Angelo died of a stroked," the news reporter said. When Kaitlin heard those words she froze and replayed it over in her head you could see her eyes swelling up with tears. Then she immediately called Violet "Hello," Violet Albert is dead I just saw it on the news," WHAT!" The sisters said going back and forth.

Violet ran over to pick Kaitlin up in her brand new black Mercedes Benz it was awesome. And they road all the way to Katie's house when they got their she was sitting on the couch crying. So the girls came over and comforted her they were all so devastated. "I, I just don't know what to do, I feel like my life has no meaning now," Katie said. "That's not true" both of the girls coincidentally said at the same time.

Kaitlin and Violet had to leave but they told Katie to call them or text them if she needed anything, anything at all. Katie said OK Kaitlin and Violet were heartbroken Albert was family but they still had no idea all the pain and trauma that Katie is going through. The girls went to their new home and thought, they cried and they thought. They cried as hard as it thunderstorm could rain. Though they cried and thought they said nothing.

Chapter 6

The Courageous Children

THAT NIGHT KAITLIN AND VIOLET barely slept. But when 6:00 came and then dad up and got ready to leave out for work. Katie didn't sleep at all she stared at the ceiling and prayed that this was all a dream. But it wasn't and she knew that, night Katie felt lonely of course she knew she had girls but she still felt like she had nothing. After work both of the girls went to check on Katie and she was planning the funeral so they helped her.

The funeral was and for Wednesday morning at 10 o'clock (It was Sunday). On Sunday morning 9 o'clock sharp Kaitlin and Violet got up and got ready, and when we got there it was all of Albert's family of course including Katie both of the girls decided to sit next to Katie at the sad funeral. "Albert wasn't amazing man and I will love him no matter what and I will never forget him he's the love of my life," Katie said in tears. After the funeral they all got something to eat. Though they said nothing when they looked in each others eyes they new what they all wanted to say.

Katie went home and Kaitlin and Violet went to their house when they got there and watch some TV and just sat in silence. When the day was over they went to sleep Kaitlin couldn't stop thinking about Albert nor Katie or Violet. That morning both of the girls got up for work. But before they left out they went to go check on Katie she was awake and of course the girls had an hour before they had to get to work. So Kaitlin and Violet told Katie that they think they should face Albert's death face forward and just push through it, by taking group counseling.

Katie thought it was an amazing idea and they scheduled appointment for Sunday (It was Thursday). By the time they were done talking Kaitlin Violet had to leave for work. Days went by everybody did what they had to do but it wasn't easy. Come Thursday Kaitlyn and Violet look up extra early so they can go show Katie Violet's new car and of course go to group counseling. When they got there they sat down and explained to the group leader along with many others what happens to the them. After counseling they all felt so much better so they decided to continue going.

After going to the counseling 2 a week for so many weeks they felt a lot better about Albert's death. So they signed out and no long went. But unfortunately when Katie, Violet, and Kaitlin stopped going to counseling Violet and Kaitlin lost touch of Katie. But one day Kaitlin and Violet saw Katie in the super market. Of course they talked and talked and talked.

And they stayed in touch for several years until Kaitlin and Violet's dad got out of prison.

So they lost touch again, but on the bright side their dad was out of prison. They were extremely happy to see him they told him all about Katie and Albert. And of course their father wanted to meet Katie said they arranged A brunch and got to know each other a lot better. "You know you girls are the most courageous children I've ever met I mean after all that I've been through that you kept pushing forward, i'm very proud of you girls," there father said. And a week later their father was in the newspaper of course because you just got out of prison but when the girls story leaked they were known as...